FORBIDDEN RIVER

BARTLETT BROTHERS
FORBIDDEN RIVER
ROGER ELWOOD

WORD
kids!

WORD PUBLISHING

Dallas · London · Vancouver · Melbourne

FORBIDDEN RIVER

Edited by Beverly Phillips.

Library of Congress Cataloging-in-Publication Data
Elwood, Roger.
     Forbidden river / Roger Elwood.
        p.   cm. — (The Bartlett brothers)
Summary: Teenage brothers Ryan and Chad find them-
selves in the midst of an international conflict filled with
terror and intrigue when their father is kidnapped by South
American drug lords.
  ISBN 0-8499-3304-8
  [1. Narcotics, Control of—Fiction. 2. Colombia—Fiction.
3. Adventure and adventurers—Fiction.] I. Title. II. Series:
Elwood, Roger. Bartlett brothers.
PZ7.E554Fo   1991
[Fic]—dc20   91-21941
                                       CIP
                                       AC

Printed in the United States of America

1 2 3 4 5 6 9 RRD 9 8 7 6 5 4 3 2 1

To
Laura Minchew
and
Beverly Phillips
—For being who they are

 # One

The White House!

Ryan Bartlett could hardly believe what was happening . . . and in such a short period of time.

Less than a week! Man, what a bombshell Dad dropped on us. We had no idea about any of it!

Ryan had always considered himself pretty much able to adjust easily to about anything. He had learned to keep his cool whatever the circumstances might be. It had been necessary with the kind of day-to-day situations his father's work had forced upon him and his brother Chad . . . and before she died, their mother.

In spite of all that, I woke up this morning and wondered if I had dreamed the whole thing, Ryan thought. *I mean, Dad's call to us, the incredible news he had announced, his solemn promise that he wasn't playing some kind of weird joke on us . . . . and then it hit Chad and me. It hit us hard about how much our lives would be changing, again! But after we talked about it, we were so excited. . . .*

There he was, in a jetliner, his brother sitting next to him. The two of them were flying to Washington, D.C., for a special ceremony that would involve their father. Andrew Bartlett was being appointed the new national security advisor to the President of the United States.

Unbelievable! Ryan told himself. *And all I could do was accuse Dad of some kind of practical joke. Wow, was I ever wrong!*

He closed his eyes, his mind going back over the past four years or so. So much had happened. First there was the death of their mother when the family car exploded. It was thought to have been caused by a bomb planted by terrorists. But later it was found to have been ordered by a Mafia godfather.

That's where the rubber hits the road, he understood as he went back over those moments. *Oh, Lord, I did forgive the man, just as I have been forgiven of the hatred I first had for him.*

And now Washington, D.C., was to be their new home.

Just a few weeks ago, Andrew Bartlett had been in the Middle East on a secret mission to uncover hidden chemical weapons. Then he was called back to the nation's capital.

"I have no idea what's going on," he had told them during a phone call as soon as he'd arrived at his hotel. "But I can say this much: I doubt that it's bad in any way."

"How do you know that?" Ryan asked, always the worrier in the family.

"Well, it's like this, son: Everybody I've seen here is smiling. Hey, after all these years, I *know* this government crowd almost as well as I do you guys. There isn't a long face among them. Believe me, with the world the way it is these days, *that* is a miracle in itself!"

The next morning, their father phoned them again. He had been told the reason behind his being called to Washington.

"The end of the month," he said, his voice full of excitement. "That's when I set up shop. Some committees need to confirm me, but that's probably not a big deal. If I've done anything right over the years, it's been to keep a good reputation. Praise God for that!"

Ryan and Chad had been so excited after they hung up the phone receiver that they both let out several wild whoops of amazement.

"We're going to be moving!" Chad had said, a big smile lighting up his face. "Back East, to . . . to—."

He couldn't finish the sentence. The words jumbled together in his throat.

Ryan couldn't speak either. The whole idea had made even the tips of his toes tingle with excitement.

National Security Advisor!

Andrew Bartlett, his dad—right next door to the President. . . .

It was something that seemed like a dream.But it was real. *They were on their way to Washington.*

"Ryan," Chad was whispering into his ear. "There's something strange going on in the cockpit."

Ryan shook his head, clearing it of his daydreams about the new position their father would soon be taking.

"What are you saying?" Ryan asked.

"Dunno. Makes me a little uncomfortable."

Ryan looked ahead, down the aisle, trying to understand what his brother was talking about.

One of the stewardesses did seem really nervous.

She was peering out from behind the cockpit door, her eyes narrowed. Ryan could see that she was frowning.

Something else.

Both brothers had been well trained by their father to pay attention to things going on around them. Their instincts were sharp, and their experiences over the last few years had taught them to trust those instincts. They could—.

Feel tension.

Feel it in the air sometimes.

See it on the faces of others.

Like now.

With the stewardess.

Especially after it seemed to Ryan that she was being *pulled* back into the cockpit!

"Chad, did you—?" he started to ask.

"Yeah, I did. I think this plane is being hijacked."

"What should we do?"

"We're just kids. What are we *supposed* to do? There're plenty of adults here. They're much better equipped than we are to do something, if there's anything wrong in the first place."

The door opened again.

A shadow.

The shadow of an object.

A certain very specific object.

. . . the shadow of a revolver!

Ryan leaned over to his brother.

"This plane has one of those new phones on it," he whispered. "I've got our credit card. I'm going back."

"Use it in the restroom," Chad told him. "That'll buy you more time, until they discover what's going on?"

"They?" Ryan repeated.

"There might be more than one, you know. It could be anybody else here on the plane."

"Even a woman."

"That's right. *Be* careful!"

Ryan nodded, stood, and walked down the aisle toward the back of the plane.

Two other stewardesses were in the galley area, trying very hard to look busy. Ryan could see that this was only an act on their part. Their movements were slow and forced, like robots, not human beings going about their normal business in a normal way.

He pointed to the phone, then nodded in the direction of the cockpit at the other end of the plane. Both stewardesses blinked twice at him, their makeshift signal of approval.

Ryan awkwardly slipped his credit card into the slot indicated. He waited for approval, then held the cordless phone close to his chest as he walked quickly to the restroom and ducked inside.

His father.

He called the hotel where his father was staying. Andrew Bartlett seldom did anything that involved them as a family without his sons' approval. That was why he hadn't already gotten a house or an apartment. That was something they would do together.

Lord, I pray that he's there, I pray that he—!

The phone in his father's room was busy.

"Would you like to wait?" the operator told him.

"No, I can't," Ryan spoke in a low, nervous voice.

6

"Break in. It's an emergency!"

"What kind of emergency?"

"I can't tell you."

"Then I can't connect you."

"Please, you've—!"

Click.

She'd hung up on him.

No! his mind screamed.

He dialed again.

A different operator—sometimes hotels had several, in order to handle the volume of calls.

"Please, ring my father, it's urgent. His name is Andrew Bartlett. Please hurry!"

"Calm down there," the operator told him soothingly. "I heard how the other operator handled your first call. I'm sorry she acted like that. By the way, you *are* the same caller, aren't you, son?"

"Yes!"

"I took the liberty of interrupting Andrew Bartlett's conversation. He's waiting for your call now."

Praise God, praise God!

His father answered after one ring.

"Dad!"

"Ryan, what's going on? I was talking to the Secretary of Defense just then. This had better be good. You should be on your way here by now. Is there some trouble with the plane you're on?"

7

"Not *with* the plane, Dad. It may be two guys or more *in* the plane! I think we're being hijacked."

Ryan told him what he and Chad had seen.

"Anything else you can tell me, son?" Mr. Bartlett asked, his words sounding strained. "Anything that might help identify those men?"

"No, that's—," Ryan started to say.

Just then the restroom door was torn nearly off its hinges.

A tall, broad-shouldered, bearded man with a gun began screaming at him. "Give me the phone, kid, or I blow your head off!"

"I love you, Dad," Ryan yelled into the receiver, before it was ripped out of his hand.

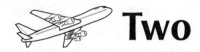 # Two

When the Secretary of Defense learned what was going on, he assured Andrew Bartlett that the CIA and any other needed agency would be giving their fullest cooperation.

"Thank you, sir," Mr. Bartlett replied, with real gratitude. "In addition, I suspect that I will need permission from you and others to take charge of this myself."

He waited for the response, realizing that going by the book was extremely important in Washington. And he knew what he was asking was very much out of the ordinary.

"Yes, I know it's unusual, but—."

He waited again.

"Thank you, sir," he said finally. "You can imagine how much the outcome means to me."

He hung up the receiver and sat on the edge of the bed in his hotel room, trembling.

My sons! On a plane with some madmen!

Andrew Bartlett had been involved in searching out terrorists for a very long time, twenty years in fact. But the worst moments of his career came nearly four years ago when his wife was killed by a group of such men. At least, for several years he had thought terrorists were responsible for her death. But then he had discovered recently that some *mafioso* henchmen were involved instead.

Even so, they were really what amounted to being terrorists of a sort, he told himself. *They tried to scare me off their trail because I was getting too close to their Middle Eastern gun sources.*

He bowed his head, not in prayer but in weariness. He was tired of living in hotel rooms in foreign countries and meeting strange people in dusty, out-of-the-way places. His life was continually in danger. He never knew when—.

First, their mother. Now, Ryan and Chad themselves. Lord, it just does not seem to end. . .

He was relieved that, at last, he would be able to work in Washington, D.C. And he was especially glad that he would now be working in the White House, down the hallway from the President of the United States! He looked forward to having a single base of operations, instead of having to set up one with each new assignment!

He realized that there would continue to be a great deal of travel, as he was called upon to negotiate with governments around the world, often at a moment's notice. But the circumstances would be different and not nearly so dangerous, and he would not be on his own so much.

They were flying here, to be with me for a few days, and then we were going back to California to finish up matters there.

He had stopped trembling, but that was all. His emotions were still stirred up.

If only I had done it differently, he thought. *If only they had left a day earlier or a day later. . . .*

He slapped his hands down on the bed, realizing how foolish he was being. Only God knew what was going to happen in the tense hours that lay ahead of them. And, as such, He must be seeing some purpose in it all, even if Andrew Bartlett and his sons couldn't.

Mr. Bartlett stood and walked over to a window in the hotel suite. He could see planes arriving at and departing from Washington National Airport in the near distance.

If only . . .

"Cut it out! Now!" he spoke out loud to the emptiness of the room in which he found himself. It was a hotel room not much different from many others he had stayed in through the years. *What you have to do, now, is concentrate on keeping your sons safe,* he told himself.

But then Andrew Bartlett also realized how little control he really did have over the situation.

Carlos Ramirez had convinced himself that he had no choice about his mission.

What other way is there? he thought again and again, before ever setting foot on that jetliner. *The powerful drug network that controls my country must be stopped. I've tried other things and . . . and nothing has worked, nothing until now. Too many innocent people are being hurt. Too many in my own country are being corrupted or killed, ending up in—.*

He hesitated to say the words, the words that carried with them sights and sounds that he could never, never forget.

Forbidden River!

The place of execution for those who rebelled against the will of the evil drug lords of his native land, the name that made brave men quiver with fear!

And our elected officials do nothing!

Ramirez felt that someone needed to make an honest statement about how corrupt the government in his country was. It was siding with the Forbidden River Drug Cartel when it should be cooperating with other nations in an effort to wipe out that organization of drug bosses.

The whole world must know what is going on, he told himself. *Our presidente is on the payroll of evil men. No one will listen to me about this unless I make news in a very big way. The decline and corruption of my country and the filth that is being exported from coca fields to the world goes on and on, killing many thousands of young people. Yes! I must act. I must make people everywhere listen!*

He considered the full extent of the scandal that he had uncovered just a few weeks earlier.

It goes beyond the land of my birth. I know why a certain U. S. senator happens to be blocking the truth from getting to the public. He has convinced some of the American president's closest advisors that I am nothing more than a Hispanic crazy man who doesn't know what he's talking about. And this has been allowed to filter out to the media. I have been labeled—.

He swallowed hard, anger and frustration and tension all constricting his throat muscles.

If everyone only knew the truth . . . if the President of the United States only realized that the chairman of a committee involved in the war against drugs is being paid off by some of the same drug lords he's supposed to be exposing. This makes him as much a criminal as the terrible men who are bribing him. They have no honor, nor does he!

There was only his friend, Roberto Estavez, and they had joined together. Ramirez knew that what they were doing was wrong. But he also was convinced that the far greater wrong was letting the evil of drugs continue . . . reaping profits for drug pushers and killing young people.

Leaving Roberto behind to stand guard over the captain and the co-pilot, he left the cockpit and stood before the seventy-six other people in that plane.

"I will tell you what we intend," he started to say. "We do not want to harm anyone. We are here on a mission of justice."

. . . . We do not want to harm anyone.

Ryan had heard that one before. And he had learned that it was usually said by people with murder on their minds.

. . . a mission of justice.

And that one, too!

Chad and he glanced at one another, indicating by their expressions that they didn't believe the hijacker at all.

I wonder if it ever occurred to this character that he doesn't gain the trust of anyone at the point of a gun!

By now, Ryan and Chad realized, their father must have been well aware of what was going on.

The jetliner's captain would have had to transmit a change of direction to avoid any mid-air collision with another aircraft in the same flight pattern.

From a straight run to Washington, D.C., we've turned south and are heading toward—.

Ryan could see that this was happening, even through the small window beside him.

"The plane's turning now," he had remarked quietly a minute or two earlier to Chad. His brother nodded in agreement as they both watched what was going on.

"Listen, . . ." Chad said, pointing to the one hijacker.

The man was speaking again.

"My friend and I . . . we have damaging information that we can't get out to the media any other way," he was saying. "Everyone we turn to either doesn't believe us or has been paid off."

One of the male passengers spoke up.

"Nonsense!" he shouted. "Just get International Press Syndicate to listen to you!"

"We tried that, mister," the hijacker told him. "The bureau chief in Los Angeles is on their payroll."

"Whose payroll?" the passenger asked. "You're not making any sense at all, young man."

That was when the hijacker told the passengers and crew on that plane his remarkable story.

His name was Carlos Ramirez; his friend Roberto Estavez was staying in the cockpit with the captain and the co-pilot. The two of them had come to the United States, hoping that they could make a better living here. Eventually they planned to bring their families to be with them. The South American country where they all had been born was in the control of the Forbidden River Drug Cartel. And officials at every level of government were "on the take," benefitting from the illegal drug activity.

Only those men and women willing to harvest the coca plant, which is used to make cocaine, shared with the government in the billions of dollars generated by selling the drug on the international market.

Other people remained every bit as poor as the Ramirez and Estavez families had been. But none of them could do anything to change the situation because of one terrible fact of life: True power was in the brutal hands of the military, the police, and the roving bands of gangsters. The gangster types were employed by the drug lords to get rid of those who got in their way, especially those the other groups missed! There was little that anyone could do.

"We could not stand it any longer," Ramirez said. "Protesters were shot or fed to the crocodiles. I remember standing at one section of the

Forbidden River and seeing the water streaked with blood."

The Forbidden River!

Ryan had heard about that one.

"Hey, didn't your own government conduct some raids on the coca fields near Forbidden River just a few months ago?" he spoke up, doubting the man's story.

"A con game," Ramirez replied, disgust on his face. "It was nothing more than an empty public relations gesture to keep suspicion away from what was really going on."

The Forbidden River district was the center of not only the coca fields but also the chemical labs run by the Cartel. It was there that the coca plant was turned into the white-powder drug used by millions of addicted customers all over the world. It was also the scene of so-called "executions" where victims were thrown into the river itself, a river that was full of hungry crocodiles!

"You talk about nobody being willing to listen," Chad said this time. "That's hard to believe."

"Yes, yes, it is," Ramirez agreed. "But that is their strength, the strength of these monsters. It is a very large part of what is protecting them to this very day. They are clever, powerful men, if you can call them men at all."

Men? Chad thought. *At least I agree with him about that. They were more like devils than human beings. They were interested only in profits, profits that were made out of the misery of drug addicts everywhere.*

"You've been in the United States for how long now?" a woman asked, with a suspicious tone.

"A year," Ramirez told her.

"Why did you wait so long? Where was your conscience six or nine months ago?"

"We could do nothing until—."

"—until your families were safe," Ryan spoke up, surprising everyone who could hear what he had said.

The hijacker smiled appreciatively.

"That's right. Roberto and I earned just enough money to bring them to Miami."

"Aren't they in danger there?" Ryan added, still trying to find some hole in the man's story.

"They're being protected by a group of our countrymen who are standing with us, side by side," replied Ramirez.

Ryan was struggling with himself. There was no doubt that he or Chad *could* help, in an instant, by getting in touch with his father in Washington D.C. But then there seemed no way he could actually risk believing what the hijacker was saying.

Ryan's entire body stiffened at the next thought: *What if this man and his friend found out that the sons of the new national security advisor to the President of the United States were on the plane? The possibilities for ransom or whatever were terrifying!*

Three

Senator Richard Bosworth was sitting at the large, expensive desk in his Washington, D.C., office when an aide knocked on the door rather hurriedly.

"Enter," Bosworth said.

The aide, a college graduate in his mid twenties, looked troubled.

"You haven't seen a ghost, have you?" the senator asked jokingly.

"No, sir, I . . . I don't believe in them," the twenty-five-year-old aide said, a lock of red hair falling down over his freckled forehead.

Jeffrey Toland had been on the senator's staff for four years. The tall, bright young man was always courteous. And Bosworth appreciated his businesslike attitude.

"Now what's so urgent?"

"This, sir."

He handed Bosworth a yellow sheet of paper.

The senator froze when he saw it.

"Sir," the aide said, a puzzled look on his face. "Now you're the one who looks like he's seen a—."

"Go!" Bosworth said sharply. "I have to study this."

The aide blushed, his cheeks nearly as red as his hair, and left, closing the door quietly behind him.

As soon as the door was shut, Bosworth read the heavily-coded message that had come over the office fax machine. It wasn't the first one like that he had received. He had told his entire staff a lie, something about top secret communications from the Pentagon. Nobody gave it a second thought after that.

He was sweating as he came to the last few words:

If something *is* wrong, they must be stopped, and quickly. . . .

Bosworth crumpled up the sheet and threw it in a waste basket at the left side of his desk. Then he just sat there, thinking sadly of the past couple of years, thinking of the step-by-step process that had grabbed at him like quicksand.

I'm drowning, he thought, gripped by panic. *I'm in over my head, and I can just barely breathe.*

Bosworth remembered that first time, that first nervous time, the sour-looking man had passed to him a plain white envelope with ten one-thousand-dollar bills in it. It had happened in a dark little restaurant. And Bosworth still remembered his guilt as he arrived home afterwards, having to pretend to his family that everything was normal.

But nothing has been normal from the moment I wrapped my fingers around that money! . . . Or any of the drugs that have flowed my way for many, many months now.

The man who contacted him had seemed so calm, so matter-of-fact.

"No big deal, Senator," he had said quite casually. "Just sit on a few Senate bills that we don't like, just keep them buried somewhere on your committee's schedule. The public tends to lose interest after a while. So do your fellow senators. Most of the bills will be forgotten. Those that aren't, well, we'll just count on your vote, among other things."

Bosworth shivered at those last three words.

. . . among other things.

Like convincing various other senators to go his way and doing so without raising any suspicions about his motives. . . . Like leaking certain news to the media so that drug dealers would be tipped off and could pass more bribes to so-called public servants in their cities and states.

But I'm as high up the ladder of government as anyone can get, he thought. *I'm their special prize. A senator is worth a dozen mayors!*

He took a key from a special compartment in his wallet, unlocked a drawer on the right side of his desk, and took out a thick file folder.

Here it all is. . . . The names and addresses of every elected official who is receiving money directly from this group of South American drug lords or their middlemen—those rotten little pushers working with them throughout the United States, selling drugs on street corners and in school yards and abandoned buildings and restrooms everywhere!

There was a world map hanging on the dark wood-paneled wall in front of him.

He knew also that the powerful influence of that handful of corrupt and evil men extended not just to America but to Europe as well. In Asia, however, the South American drug runners had competition from equally cruel Oriental sources.

"I'm part of it," he said verbally. "I'm—."

Senator Richard Bosworth couldn't stop his stomach from trembling or his hands from shaking.

24

 # Four

"**A** respected United States senator is at the very center of this whole lousy mess!"

Carlos Ramirez's words seemed frozen in the air, with everyone looking at them with disbelief as he stood at the front of the plane, his partner still in the cockpit.

"Which one?" Ryan asked, still without being convinced.

"Richard Bosworth!"

Ryan definitely had heard that name before. His father mentioned Bosworth when there was some discussion of international drug smuggling.

The senator is chairman of the committee that is overseeing the government's war against drugs!

"Did the Forbidden River Cartel get to him somehow?" Ryan dared to speak up, again.

"Yeah, they did," Ramirez acknowledged. "The respected senator had a secret cocaine habit. It had become so bad that it was costing him a great deal of money, hundreds of dollars *a day!* He knew he couldn't keep piling up that kind of debt. So they just erased it off their books, gave him all the cocaine he wanted, and they figured they had bought him as a result."

Governmental influence up for grabs!

Ryan wondered what kind of mess his father was really getting into. He knew that Andrew Bartlett had far too much integrity ever to sell his own ethics down the river, Forbidden River or otherwise. If anyone ever tried to bribe him, Ryan smiled proudly, they would be setting a trap for themselves and no one else!

Ryan leaned back, studying Ramirez a little more closely this time without automatically thinking that he was a liar.

Carlos Ramirez was in his mid twenties, a blond-haired Hispanic, certainly a rare trait for someone of his nationality. His face was clean-shaven, and he was dressed in a colorful sport shirt and fashion jeans.

Another passenger, a thin-faced man who seemed to be in his mid fifties, spoke up at this point.

"If you will put down the gun, I think we could make some progress here," he said slowly, deliberately.

"And why should I listen to you?" Ramirez asked.

"I happen to be a senator also."

"And you're telling me this, knowing that I could easily use you as a bargaining chip?" Ramirez asked.

"I know people, young man. I can spot professional types a mile away," the senator told him.

"And so you think I don't do this for a living then?"

"I doubt it."

"What makes you such an expert?" Ramirez asked.

"I told you I'm a senator. That's true . . . Ramon Torres of New Mexico. My brother is Miguel Torres, special ambassador to Colombia."

"He helped to get several of the drug kingpins extradited to the United States for trial," Ramirez remarked.

"Correct. I'm going to be nominated as the new head of the U.S. Drug Enforcement Agency and plan to have Miguel recalled from Colombia in order to work with me. I will be pleased to work with the new National Security Advisor who has expressed a desire to be as helpful as possible."

Dad!

Chad's eyes shot wide open.

He's talking about Dad!

He nudged his brother who nodded with at least the same amount of concern.

Chad closed his eyes.

Lord, we need Your help now as much as we ever have. Show us what to do or say. Guide us both. Give us the wisdom we need now.

When he opened his eyes, he saw something quite remarkable.

Ramirez had lowered his gun.

"But what can we do?" he asked. "You are just one man. This enemy is powerful. They have spies everywhere."

Senator Torres stood and cautiously walked up the aisle toward the other man.

"You may find this difficult to accept, but I must tell you that *some* people *can* be trusted even in this world of ours today."

Ryan shot to his feet.

"My father is—," he started to say.

Everyone in the passenger's cabin turned toward Ryan, including Senator Torres and Ramirez.

Lord, he thought prayerfully, *is this what You want me to be doing right now?*

His mouth felt dry, as though he had been out in a desert, and his throat seemed to be almost paralyzed.

"My father's the one—," Ryan tried again, "you mentioned a few minutes ago. He's—."

His heart was pounding as he forced the words out.

 # Five

Richard Bosworth's aide, Jeffrey Toland, slipped into a phone booth several blocks from the Senate Office Building in Washington, D.C., where he had worked for the senator for nearly two years.

I've got to do something, he thought. *I can't continue to pretend that nothing's going on. Too many mysterious—.*

Characters.

There was no other word to describe some of the visitors to that office. They often came after business hours, and most of the other members of Bosworth's staff had already left.

I'm always the one to work later than anybody in their right mind, Toland recalled. *If I hadn't been so dedicated, I would never have seen anything, at least not enough to become suspicious.*

At first he ignored the men, thinking them to be simply some rough types who wanted help from their elected public servant. He never imagined anything illegal was going on.

Trust. . . .

That's what he tried not to let go of. In fact, he had hung onto his trust in the man as long as he could. But—

All earthly idols have feet of clay. . . .

Toland wasn't sure if that phrase happened to be derived from some portion of the Bible or not. Whatever the case, he came to realize how real it was, especially in the case of Senator Richard Bosworth.

The senator doesn't know that I accidently cracked his secret code months ago. So I knew what that message was today even if he thinks that I didn't.

He repeated the words in his mind:

If something *is* wrong, they must be stopped, and quickly. . . .

By itself that message was hardly very scary. But when it was linked in with others, it formed a paper trail that was as damaging to the senator as it was dangerous to the security of the United States.

One fortunate detail, he admitted to himself. *I have all sorts of contacts now. One of the most recent is with Andrew Bartlett.*

Toland started to dial the special number that he had obtained more than ten months earlier. Of course, he had never expected that he would actually be using it.

Andrew Bartlett . . . one of the intelligence community's best men!

Toland wished he could have gotten to know the man personally. From what he had been able to learn, Andrew Bartlett had his share of basic faults, like any human being. But he was certain that one of them was not a willingness to sell out his country along with hundreds of thousands of drug addicts in every state across the nation.

A voice answered.

"Is this Andrew Bartlett, sir?" Toland asked nervously.

"It isn't."

"Can you tell me how to get ahold of him?"

"Try the White House."

"Why there?"

"Andrew Bartlett is soon to be installed as the next national security advisor to the President."

Toland's mouth dropped open.

That means he can accomplish more now than ever before. I've got to make contact with him!

"It's an emergency, sir," he said into the telephone receiver. "Can you please help me?"

Pause.

He could hear some discussion in the background, as though the man who had answered had placed a palm over the receiver and was talking to someone else.

Finally—.

"Where are you now?" Toland was asked.

"At a phone booth several blocks from the Senate Office Building."

"Give me your number. I could contact Bartlett if you let me have your name and tell me just a little of what you want him for."

Toland read off the phone number then:

"I'm Jeffrey Toland, aide to Senator Richard Bosworth."

"Go on."

"He's—."

Toland was trembling.

"What's wrong?" the other man asked.

Toland was thinking how he had stumbled across a strange file in the Senator's office . . . how he had copied the names, addresses, and phone numbers of other public officials on the take from the drug lords. He was also thinking about the pile of decoded messages that he had gathered together over the months.

"I—I have proof that Bosworth is on the payroll of some—."

Toland saw a dark green sedan pull into a parking space across the street. Two big men got out, pretending not to be looking at him. But Toland instantly saw through their act and shouted into the receiver. "They're after me. I'm going to head out of here. I'll take—."

How could they have found out that I was on to them? Bosworth himself couldn't be aware of what I've been doing. Someone must have figured that it was strange for me to be working late at the office as often as I was. Someone put two and two together, and it all added up to suspicion about me. They probably haven't even told Bosworth as yet. . . .

Toland hurriedly gave the approximate route he thought he could take as he tried to escape. He replaced the receiver and picked up his briefcase. Then acting as casually as possible, he opened the door of the phone booth and started to walk down the street, glancing out of the corner of his eye at the two men who hadn't made it across the street as yet.

This is one time I'm grateful for all this Washington, D.C., traffic!

As soon as Jeffrey Toland had reached the next corner, he turned right and started running.

When Andrew Bartlett received the phone call from headquarters, he couldn't believe that they had bothered him.

"My sons are on a hijacked plane, and you're calling about a senator who's supposed to be crooked," he shouted into the phone, his nerves worn thin.

The plane his sons were on had changed course two times. Originally it had been headed for Washington, D.C. Then it had turned toward South America! But now it had suddenly shifted course again and was apparently headed toward Washington, D.C., once more.

As soon as Mr. Bartlett had spoken so harshly, he stopped himself, got his thoughts back together, and apologized.

"No problem, Andy," the agent at the other end said. "What do you want to do about this?"

"I really shouldn't—," Mr. Bartlett started to say.

Then something clicked in his mind.

Richard Bosworth . . . chairman of a crucial senate committee on the drug problem . . . a plane being hijacked and heading toward South America . . . then mysteriously turning around and . . . and, finally, that last stunning message from one of the hijackers:

"My friend and I must be given a guarantee of protection. There are terrible men in your government who have been paid off by the drug lords. Our lives are in danger. You must help us!"

He repeated that second sentence.

There are terrible men in your government who have been paid off by the drug lords.

"I'm on the way now," Andrew Bartlett said. "I'll be there in less than five minutes."

He knew an agency car was waiting for him, with an armed fellow agent ready to take him where he wanted to go.

In a few seconds they were heading toward the spot from which the senator's aide had been calling.

Too much time had passed.

Mr. Bartlett had been worried about that from the moment he started tracing the route given by the aide.

He's probably dead by now. In eleven minutes anything could—!

"Look!" the other agent yelled. The young, blond-haired man named Randolph Atkins was pointing toward an all-night convenience store on the right.

The front window had been completely knocked out; glass was strewn over the pavement.

Inside, two extremely rough-looking men, big enough to be football stars, were dragging a smaller man toward the back door.

"Could we be thinking the same thing?" Atkins said knowingly.

"We could, and I bet we are!" Mr. Bartlett replied.

Atkins pulled the agency car over to the curb just in front of the convenience store.

They had to act quickly for there to be any hope at all of saving the young aide.

"You down the alley!" Mr. Bartlett told Atkins. "I'll head in through the store."

Atkins nodded and proceeded toward the alley.

Mr. Bartlett saw a mess when he entered the store: milk cartons burst open, eggs smashed against the floor, boxes of donuts and cookies scattered about.

And a terrified man huddled behind the counter.

The name tag on his shirt indicated he was the store manager. He sat there too dazed to move, fruit punch splashing down on him from the counter above.

The back door was ajar.

Mr. Bartlett approached it carefully, trying not to make any noise. He peered around the edge of the door. To his right, he saw that the three other men had entered an alley with no outlet, a dead end.

One of them was holding the aide while the other pounded him in the stomach.

Mr. Bartlett could see a pile of papers and a manila folder in the free hand of the one who was swinging again and again at the aide.

"Hands up! *Way* up!" Mr. Bartlett said as he jumped out into the alley. "We're Federal officers! Make a move toward any weapon, and you're dead where you stand!"

Neither of the two men seemed to believe what he had said. The one holding the young aide suddenly dropped him and reached for a gun of his own. Mr. Bartlett shot him in the shoulder. The impact was so powerful that it knocked the man against a group of trash cans, scattering the contents in every direction.

The other man managed to get his own revolver out and was aiming it at Mr. Bartlett. Normally Agent Bartlett would have had no problem disarming the man. But at that very moment he realized—

My own gun! It's jammed!

Mr. Bartlett could do nothing.

The second man smiled cruelly and aimed his weapon at Mr. Bartlett's head.

The sound of another shot echoed through the alley.

The second man's mouth opened and shut in pain as he, too, was knocked off his feet.

Mr. Bartlett jerked his head around. Agent Atkins was standing there, looking more than a little pale, his left cheek twitching.

"Your first time?" Andrew Bartlett asked as the two of them ran quickly to the nearly unconscious aide.

Atkins nodded, clearly embarrassed.

"Is it that obvious?" he asked.

"As it was with me the first time, son."

 # Six

Carlos Ramirez had handed over his weapon minutes earlier, and so had his friend Roberto Estavez.

"We're so sorry," Estavez said as he stood at the front of the airliner's passenger compartment, knowing that everyone was studying him but for a much different reason this time. "We were just so confused. We were never going to hurt anyone."

"I know how you must feel," Senator Ramon Torres assured him. "None of that will keep you out of prison, and yet—."

He rubbed his chin with his left hand for a few seconds before he called Ryan and Chad up front with him. They gulped a couple of times and then joined him.

"I am one of your father's admirers," Torres told them. "Could he be of some help to us in this matter?"

"Help?" Ryan asked. "How, sir?"

"I suspect that Andrew Bartlett has resources even a senator such as myself just does not have."

"I think he would really try his best."

Torres nodded, then turned to the two former hijackers.

"I can't promise probation or anything of the sort. I would be laughed out of Congress if I tried to get anything like that started. But, Carlos, if you have the kind of information you are claiming, well, Andrew Bartlett is the first one you need to talk with. That is, after you spend some time, of course, with certain Federal officers."

"The FBI?" Ramirez asked.

"Yes, and others."

"Can they protect us?"

"I think so."

"You can't imagine how deeply the Forbidden River Cartel has burrowed itself into the very fabric of your American democratic society," Estavez added nervously. His knowledge gave him reason to wonder what the future held. "Do you remember a movie a few years ago called *Invasion of the Body Snatchers?*"

"I remember it well," Torres admitted. "Are you saying that the drug lords in your country are as expert at concealing themselves as were the aliens in that film?"

Estavez nodded as he said, "I hate to say it, but they're *more* expert, senator, a *lot* more. The aliens were trying to pretend that they were human beings, and that left them open to being tracked down because sometimes they wouldn't get it right. But with the Cartel . . . well, *their* agents *are* human, and they fit in much, much better."

Torres rubbed his right arm with his left hand.

"Are you okay, sir?" Ryan asked.

"Yes, yes, I am, but I'm beginning to get a hunch here."

He lowered his voice as he looked at the passengers who were trying to eavesdrop without being too obvious about it.

"What's that?" Ryan asked.

"Something the Bible warns about."

"Wickedness in high places, senator?" Chad offered.

"Exactly, my young friend," the senator remarked. "It's not every teenager who would know something like that."

"Mom and Dad raised us to believe in the Bible, to accept it as God's Word. It's part of our life."

"I'm glad to hear that," Torres said. "These *are* wicked days, Chad, and having an anchor is—."

He stopped for a moment, trying to control himself.

"It's disgusting," Ramirez said, "how some people think money can buy anything."

"Or anybody," Estavez added, knowing better

than most of the passengers in that jetliner what he was talking about.

After getting clearance, Andrew Bartlett took Jeffrey Toland to a special room *under* the White House. As it turned out, the young man had only a few bruises and sore muscles. And he was anxious to tell what he knew about the Drug Cartel.

I've been put in complete charge of the hijacking crisis as well as the investigation into Bosworth's drug connections, Mr. Bartlett thought, his mind very much on Ryan and Chad. *And I've not officially been sworn in to my new job!*

"Don't we need to act fast to stop Senator Bosworth before he does something drastic?" Toland asked.

"Until he discovers that you know what you know, there's no reason for him to act in any weird manner. You photocopied everything, didn't you? The originals are where they're supposed to be?"

"That's right. But you didn't answer my question, sir. Shouldn't we tell others the details?"

"I have to be certain that there *is* a real case against someone such as Richard Bosworth. He's big-time, as you know already. He must have set up all kinds of escape routes for himself.

Remember, Jeff, I've been at this game for a great deal longer than you have.

"Frankly I suspect that I could pretty much predict his first move when he discovers that his activities have been exposed at last. His type lives in fear of that happening, though most of them will never admit this."

Toland blushed.

"Sorry, sir. I didn't mean to sound critical."

"You're entitled. If what you have here is half as damaging as you've claimed, my friend, you just may have unearthed the most stunning scandal since Watergate. Now let's look at what you have in that file."

The phone rang.

Mr. Bartlett's hand flashed toward the receiver and lifted it to his ear.

"What's your latest?" he asked.

He listened to what the individual at the other end said, smiled broadly, thanked him, and hung up.

"The plane will soon be landing in Washington D.C.," he said joyously.

"What are you talking about, sir?" Toland asked.

"Sorry. I'm so involved, well, I guess I thought the whole world knew about the hijacking."

Mr. Bartlett explained what had happened and, also, about his sons, Ryan and Chad.

"I feel so ignorant," Toland admitted. "I didn't know about your appointment to national security advisor until today, either."

"No wonder, Jeffrey. Look at what has been happening in your own life. You haven't had time for much else, especially over the past few hours!"

Toland started handing him the different pieces of the "puzzle" he'd been able to put together.

"This one's especially interesting," he said, handing Mr. Bartlett a thick manila folder labeled *FORBIDDEN RIVER.*

"Jeffrey, first just tell me everything you know about this."

"As you already know, Forbidden River forms a western boundary to the main area of coca plant cultivation and cocaine manufacturing. A great deal of land is involved. The Drug Cartel got its name from that river."

"Forbidden River is a dangerous place."

"From what I've learned in these files and the messages I decoded, it certainly is. It's a place where the drug lords dispose of a lot of what they consider to be 'garbage'."

"Crocodiles eat up every piece, I bet."

"You're right, sir. It seems as though the victims of the Cartel are beaten badly, then thrown into Forbidden River."

"These guys have no humanity left except toward

their families," said Mr. Bartlett. "Trouble is, they're able to justify any crime as an attempt to buy security for their loved ones. How deceived can you get?"

"You have no idea, sir."

Mr. Bartlett looked at Toland and said, "Actually I do, my friend. I very much do. You see . . . these men are just another example of evil. And I have seen all kinds of evil in my job."

"By evil, do you mean they're possessed . . . possessed by Satan?"

"Who knows? Bartlett said. "If not directly possessed, then chained to his every wish, his every command."

"Sir, this file is full of people whose lives have been ruined by drugs, every one of them the victim of men who care only about the profits they are making," Toland said.

"I've seen it happen again and again, Jeffrey. Families are torn apart. Human beings become like wild animals, doing anything imaginable in order to keep themselves supplied with drugs: crack, heroin, whatever the substance was that happened to be dominating their lives."

"Yes, and I understand that LSD and magic mushrooms are making a comeback," said Toland. "Those things are terrifying. Years ago, I tried some 'special' dried mushrooms. I nearly died, sir. I attempted at one point to pull my own eyes out

45

so that I wouldn't 'see' what I thought I had been 'seeing.'"

"They were visions straight from hell."

Mr. Bartlett was thinking of Ryan and Chad then. They had never been "into" drugs, but now they were facing a very real danger that was, in fact, drug-related in an entirely different way.

For a moment he became lost in his thoughts, thoughts too personal to express to anyone.

"Sir?" Jeffrey Toland said.

"Sorry. I was just thinking. . . ."

In the next few minutes, Mr. Bartlett did his best to tell this young stranger just a little of what was weighing so heavily on him at that moment.

"I know how you feel," Toland said. "I help out at a rehab unit here in town. I see what addicts go through trying to kick their habits. And every time I think of drug dealers riding around in Cadillacs and Jaguars and Mercedes, I want to join the CIA or the FBI and go after the men who get rich by ruining other people's lives."

Mr. Bartlett began to look through the folder Toland handed to him. Before long he came to a list of names, and suddenly his hand started shaking.

"Are you all right, sir?" Toland asked.

"Yes . . . yes . . . I am," Mr. Bartlett assured him. "Just angry, terribly, terribly angry."

What he was looking at was a computerized list, everything carefully put in alphabetical order.

It was a very long list, a very long and terrifying list of names, addresses, and phone numbers.

Men and women across the United States.

Mayors. Governors. Police chiefs. All were people who were *supposed* to be serving the public. But there were more: Company presidents. Little League sponsors. Savings-and-loan chairmen.

Hundreds of names.

All violating the trust of people who depended upon them

All being bribed by the drug lords of South America!

 # Seven

Everyone on board had breathed a sigh of relief when they learned that the jetliner was back on its original flight plan.

"We'll be in our new hometown in a couple of hours," Chad said, leaning comfortably back against his seat.

"Yeah, great," Ryan replied. "I hear there's a really terrific gym just a few blocks away from where we'll be living until we find a house."

"And *I* hear the biggest computer store in the area is right next door to it!" Chad countered, teasing his computer-whiz brother.

"Very funny," Ryan admitted. "You got me there."

He closed his eyes for a minute, then opened them again and tapped his brother on the shoulder.

"You were kidding, weren't you?" he asked.

"Go to sleep, little brother," Chad told him.

Ryan pretended to be huffy, but he didn't mean it. And he knew he wasn't at all convincing. He cared a lot about Chad, and he knew his athletic brother felt the same way about him.

Hey, Ryan thought, *with my brains and his body, we've gotten ourselves out of some pretty tight places.*

He decided to try and get some sleep.

Senator Richard Bosworth could hardly believe what the voice over the phone receiver was telling him.

"On the same plane as Andrew Bartlett's kids?" he asked again, hoping that somehow he had misunderstood.

"That's right," the deep voice growled, with obvious impatience.

"How can you be sure?"

"He thinks his friend is with him in this idiotic matter. But he's going to be real disturbed when he finds out that this isn't true!"

"Wait a minute! Roberto Estavez is on your payroll? I didn't see his name on the list."

"Not *everyone* is there. The errand boys, the two-bit grunts, we don't bother with them so much. They're a dime a dozen, Boz. They're scum we can pick up off any street."

"Not big fish like me."

"You said it. Now, listen, you'd better hope that that air-traffic controller is on duty tonight. How soon can you find out?"

"Take me five minutes," Bosworth replied. But he wasn't certain that he could deliver so quickly, and he hoped the other man wouldn't pick up on how nervous he was.

"If he isn't, then we'll have to have one of our Maryland boys go in by private plane."

"Hundreds of people could be killed."

"Sometimes the price *is* high, Boz."

"What happens to the controller?"

"He'll be fired. There'll be an investigation, but by then he'll have disappeared," the other man replied.

"You'd kill your own man."

"No. He'll be living in luxury where none of the Feds can get ahold of him. We *reward* our faithful co-workers. Remember that."

"Why don't you call this man yourself?" Bosworth asked. "You know him far better than I do. After all, you're the guy who hired him in the first place. Why make me do it?"

"*I* couldn't get through, but *you*, you're a hotshot senator. *That's* another story. You bet it is!"

"I'll do what I can."

"If you don't, *we* will."

Bosworth hung up the receiver, his mind whirling.

They think they can get me to do anything, he thought. *They think they can get me to call an air-traffic controller, someone who happens to be in their pocket, and have him give "special" landing instructions to an incoming jetliner's pilot, and cause the plane to crash-land somewhere. If I don't, they'll send in a private plane to do the job!*

He buried his head in his hands, sobbing.

Moments later, his cheeks still wet, Bosworth reached for the phone on his desk.

They think they own every inch of me!

Bosworth started dialing a certain number slowly. He dreaded the moment when the man he was calling would actually answer at the other end. And he hesitated before depressing that final number, considering once again the disaster that would likely happen in just under two hours.

They think they own—.

"This is Senator Richard Bosworth. I must speak to Juan Valez immediately!"

"One moment, Senator. Please hold."

"Juan Valez here," another voice answered, the sounds of jetliners in the background.

"Listen, Juan. And, I mean, listen good. I have a message from our South American friends."

United States Senator Richard Bosworth quickly gave instructions to the man at the other end of the line.

"Strange," Captain Jim Gibbs remarked after repeating the bizarre instructions he'd just received from an air-traffic controller at Dulles International Airport outside Washington, D.C. "It goes against everything I would have thought was correct. And the guy seemed so nervous, well, I wonder what's going on here, Artie."

"I agree with you," his co-pilot, Artie Brooks, responded. "Why do they want us to go out of our way that much?"

"Who knows?" Gibbs added. "He must have some information that we don't know about."

The expression on his face indicated that he wasn't sure of his own explanation. And not *knowing* the answer was a little upsetting to this veteran pilot.

"But you just said it's strange," Brooks persisted. "If that's what your gut feelings tell you, shouldn't we be checking this out, Captain?"

Gibbs hesitated as he considered what his co-pilot, a man he respected immensely, had just said.

Artie's got good instincts, he thought, with appreciation. *Maybe I'd better listen to him.*

By reflex, after getting flight pattern instructions from the controller, Gibbs had already started to change course. But he put everything on hold as he called back to the landing tower.

"This is AWA flight 204," he said into the microphone. "I wonder if I got the right message from you. Would you mind verifying?"

"Captain Gibbs, it was correct," the controller said, with a touch of anger. "Please, you must follow directions in order to avoid any difficulty."

Gibbs and Brooks glanced at one another, both having noticed the strained tone in the man's voice.

"Roger and out," the captain said. He broke the connection and turned quickly to the other man.

"It's your call," Brooks told him. "After all, you're the captain, old chap."

"I vote for a change of airport altogether," Gibbs replied. "Let's contact National. Tell them we're having some sort of problem communicating with Dulles. See if they have any flight patterns that would be open to us. And tell them to hurry because I'm not comfortable with the amount of fuel we have left."

"One other thing, Jim," Brooks said.

"What's that?"

"Runways. Make sure our runway is clear. We don't want what happened to flight 223 last year to happen to us."

Massive chaos . . . two planes colliding . . . many fatalities . . . scores of injured passengers.

"And runways," the captain agreed.

Juan Valez saw what was happening. Flight 204 was disregarding his instructions. He couldn't get Captain Gibbs to listen to him.

He excused himself for a moment and went hurriedly downstairs to use an isolated pay phone there.

"Yes, yes, I know," he said into the receiver. "But there is only one other thing I can try to do."

A pause.

"Get another plane to intersect their flight path," he said, his voice trembling.

Another pause.

"Yes, *I know!* But, as you said earlier, all of us could be destroyed if anyone on that plane lives. Even a crash won't guarantee anything. But there's no alternative."

Senator Richard Bosworth objected, but Juan Valez hung up on him.

Roberto Estavez had continued to hope he'd

fooled everyone with his passionate words against the men heading up the Forbidden River Cartel.

The aliens in the movie had tried to pretend that they were human beings, and that left them open to being tracked down because, sometimes, they wouldn't get it right. But with the Cartel, well, their agents are human, and they fit in much, much better.

He repeated those last words to himself.

. . . . and they fit in much, much better.

Careful that no one saw him, he smiled because he knew how true that was. He knew that his bosses could count on him to fit in, to be accepted by the other side, and never be detected.

They want Carlos dead. But the act of his murder cannot be traced back to them. Without question, it has to look like the U.S. citizens are responsible. Then the members of the Cartel would spread the news to all of Central and South America and elsewhere. They will say that the people in the United States not only want to destroy the livelihood of poor people trying to build a better life for themselves but, also, the people themselves.

Estavez could picture the rallies, the men standing up and working the crowds into an anti-U.S.A. frenzy.

"The gringos care nothing about you, about any of you. They have all the money. And they want to

take away yours, what little you have, so that you will always be like slaves to them.

"But they won't stop there, you know. Get in their way, and you're dead! They will toss you aside like your children's old toys, just as they did with Carlos Ramirez. They may condemn what we do at Forbidden River, but they have their own ways of dealing with anyone who is Hispanic."

A martyr.

That was what Carlos Ramirez would become.

I will make him proof that the Cartel is right, that the United States wants nothing less than domination over all Hispanic peoples.

He chuckled to himself about how well everything was turning out.

Now, with the hijacking charges against us, this may be even easier.

In a day or a week, however long it requires, I will take the life of my "friend" Carlos, and then escape with the right inside help. The Cartel has promised that they will reward me quite handsomely.

Roberto Estavez, very self-satisfied, very pleased with himself, would continue in his warped daydream for the next twenty minutes or so.

Then, suddenly, painfully, he would realize how wrong he had been.

Dead wrong.

 # Eight

Richard Bosworth was covered with perspiration, in spite of the sharp coolness of the weather outside.

There could be as many as 300 people involved with both planes! It was a terrifying thought, and it was forcing his stomach into a tight knot. *But if I blow the whistle on the drug people who have been paying me for special favors the past few years, my own life is over!*

Bosworth stood, paced his inner office a few times, and then left the suite altogether. He walked down the corridor, then out onto the sidewalk in front of the Senate Office Building.

Five terms as senator . . . all those years!

He breathed in deeply.

I love everything about this crazy city. I love the wild pace. I love the ever-present power. I love knowing that my actions here can have consequences that reach around the world.

But he knew he had come to "love" something else far more. Perhaps *love* wasn't the right word, under the circumstances.

Cocaine.

Just a few times at parties led to a few times in my office. Then that led to a few more times at home, then in jetliner restrooms, anywhere I could sneak some of that white powder.

Tens of thousands of dollars down the drain.

His wife Jennifer had left him months earlier. The "official" explanation was that she had gone away for a while due to a personal health problem. Actually she had gone to a clinic outside Gstaad, Switzerland, to calm her nerves; living with a cocaine addict was nerve wracking for anyone.

"Someday you won't be so clever at keeping the news from the outside world," she warned prophetically. "Someday everything will cave in on you, Richard, and you'll suddenly realize that you have no one, absolutely no one by your side anymore."

Even now, standing outside the building where he had worked for so long, he felt the compulsive urge to snort some cocaine. He was still a slave to this white-powder enemy that had been masquerading as a friend.

But another, overriding nightmare had just surfaced, competing for every bit of his attention.

The passengers and crews of two jetliners will soon collide in mid air, with no probable survivors as a result!

Bosworth began to feel very sick. The street was spinning wildly before his eyes. He hurried back into the Senate Office Building. He made it to the restroom in his office suite just in time.

Andrew Bartlett had read everything supplied by Jeffrey Toland from the secret files kept by Senator Richard Bosworth.

It's the biggest single catch I've ever seen, he thought. *I can't think of any other that compares!*

"With this, we can practically shut down the entire Cartel, Jeff," he said out loud. "We're finally going to put some of these greedy, immoral men behind bars."

"That *will* help, sure it will . . . *until* they regroup and bribe yet another set of officials," Toland reminded him. "They aren't known for giving up. And I don't think they are about to change the way they do business even one little bit. But I know we can't let that stop us. If we do, they'll have won the final victory, and that just can't be allowed to happen under *any* circumstances. These guys have to be fought again and again."

"You sound as though you should be working in national security!" Mr. Bartlett told him sincerely.

"Why don't you consider it? You're bright, young, dedicated. I could help you cut through some red tape."

When Toland saw that Mr. Bartlett was quite serious, his expression brightened for a moment. Then it turned gloomy again, making him look and feel considerably older than he was.

"It's a great idea, sir. But it all seems useless. If I could just believe that I could do some good, that even these files could accomplish something . . ."

"I understand how you feel. And you're right about the Drug Cartel. They will never change. Their crimes will simply be continued by other people who have no conscience.

"But, in the short term, Jeffrey, it *will* slow Forbidden River enterprises down. And they will lose several billion dollars."

The aide was really pleased by that prospect.

"Take away huge chunks of the fortune they've been piling up, and we'll have them howling bloody murder!" said Mr. Bartlett. "And, I say anything that hits them hard is good news."

Jeffrey eagerly agreed.

"It also will mean perhaps ten thousand fewer deaths from drug overdoses or weakened immune systems or whatever," Mr. Bartlett continued. "That's the part that I truly look forward to, Jeffrey."

"So do I," Toland remarked, "particularly after finding out about what has happened to a once fine man like Senator Bosworth."

Mr. Bartlett patted Jeffrey on the shoulder just like he would have done with his sons.

The phone rang.

Mr. Bartlett grabbed the receiver.

Blood drained immediately from his face as he learned who was calling and what the call was about.

"Are you willing to stay there until some agents can come by, Senator Bosworth?" he asked coldly after several minutes of listening. "Can I trust you to do that, Senator Bosworth?"

Mr. Bartlett listened to what the man was saying and then added, "All right, they'll be there in a few minutes."

Immediately after ending the call, he phoned someone at the agency, made the arrangements, and hung up.

Then Mr. Bartlett turned away, not able to face even Toland for a number of moments. The veins stood out on his forehead and down his neck.

"My sons!" he said his voice full of emotion. "My sons are on a plane that has been given a death sentence by madmen—men for whom human life is as disposable as toilet paper. Ryan and Chad will be dead within the next thirty minutes unless I can do something to stop it in time."

Jeffrey Toland thought he could hear Andrew Bartlett choking back some tears.

Ryan and Chad saw the lights of Dulles International Airport; then, abruptly, the jetliner changed directions.

The two brothers had been on enough flights over the years to realize that something unusual was going on.

An announcement over the loudspeaker system gave the official explanation: "Air traffic has forced us to land at National instead of Dulles. We regret that our present fuel level will not allow us to continue circling our original destination."

They were sitting directly in back of Ramirez and Estavez. Ryan was able to see through the separation between the two seats that the former hijackers had turned sharply and looked at one another. Then both stood and walked quickly toward the front of the cabin where they began talking with one of the stewardesses.

"Something's wrong," Ryan whispered to his brother, a nervous edge to his voice. He nodded toward the little scene directly ahead.

Her face deeply lined, tense-looking, the stewardess used an intercom transmitting directly to the captain's headset. After a few seconds, he came out of the cockpit and listened to the two men.

"This has happened before," Chad reminded him. "Don't panic all of a sudden. We have no idea what they're talking about. It could be something really simple. Chill out!"

Ryan was annoyed; sure, he overreacted sometimes, but this time it was different, especially after what the same men had put everyone through.

"Look at them!" he insisted. "Those guys really act as though somebody's just slapped the two of them hard across their faces."

"They're worried," Chad offered, keeping his voice not much above a whisper. "Remember, neither of them has any idea what's ahead. How would you and I feel in their shoes."

Just the same probably, Ryan admitted to himself, *maybe even a lot worse than they seem.*

"They're putting their trust and their lives into the hands of strangers," Chad continued. "It's not going to be easy for either one of those guys, believe that, Ryan. And now, on top of everything else, they're not even going to land at the same airport that they thought would be their destination. Naturally they're going to be suspicious."

Ryan rubbed his chin for a moment.

"Yeah," he agreed finally. "It must be awful as they think over the mess they've gotten themselves into now."

"Right," Chad told him. "Now you're thinking straight. It could be that they won't be punished, or maybe they *will* be given a heavy prison sentence. It could go either way for them, Ryan. Of course, they're going to be worried."

Ryan nodded, smiling a bit. Now he was thinking of their father and wondering what part he would play in a situation like that one.

For him, this kind of stuff is probably routine, he thought quite proudly. *Dad's been dealing with hijackings and terrorism and kidnappings for a long time now.*

"I hope Dad can help them, Chad," he said, "I hope he will be able to do something to—."

He turned to the window, enjoying as always the sight of countless numbers of lights twinkling in the darkness.

Even the worst places look almost like something out of fairy tales when seen at night from the air, he thought.

He fell back against the seat, his nerves calming down a bit, his head still turned toward the window.

A plane.

His eyes shot open.

"Chad, look at how close it is!" he said. "I've never seen another plane so close!"

His brother leaned over him to look outside.

"Sure is," Chad agreed. "If I didn't know better, I'd say that it was heading straight into our flight pattern."

"Shouldn't be a problem though," Ryan rambled on, trying to convince himself as much as his brother. "After all, they've got the best air-traffic controllers here. They *have* to, you know. Too many important people from dozens of different countries live in and around Washington. Accidents here can affect the whole world."

But now it was his older brother's turn to start sounding alarmed, *very* alarmed.

"Ryan, it's not altering course!" he said, raising his voice more than he intended.

Other passengers on that side of the plane happened to be noticing the same thing.

Abruptly the jetliner swerved to one side.

Not enough.

The other plane, much smaller and older, hit the big jet's right wing. It sheered off at least a third of it and smashed in its own cockpit section at the same time.

Less than a minute later both planes would crash into the residential area directly below.

 # Nine

Senator Richard Bosworth waited for the government agents to arrive. He stood in the middle of his inner office looking at the plaques and photographs that took up every inch of wood-paneled wall space.

"So outstanding a career," he said out loud. "And so many people have thought me to be a symbol of decency and integrity."

He started laughing at that, not a good laugh, not a laugh of joyous relief, but a laugh of bitterness and regret. It was the kind of laughter that comes just before a very loud cry of deep sorrow.

That cry came next.

He fell to his knees.

"I feel so naked," he moaned. "I feel so empty."

Everything that he had become would soon be open for inspection by the world outside the privacy of that office.

The media will gobble up all the terrible, ugly details. They'll try to get to my family, my psychiatrist, the members of my staff, anyone who has ever had anything to do with me!

The phone rang.

At first he did not answer it. It was as though he were in the midst of a dream, and if he ignored the ringing phone long enough, it really would go away.

It didn't.

The phone kept on ringing.

Bosworth stumbled over to the phone on his desk, picked up the receiver, and mumbled "Hello."

A familiar, thickly-accented and quite harsh voice said, "The planes are down. We have men headed toward the scene now. Some are posing as paramedics and others as so-called 'innocent' bystanders. Two more will pretend to have been on one of the planes."

"Aren't you satisfied?" Bosworth said, nearly shouting into the receiver. "You've caused an awful disaster. It's nothing less than a mass murder. What more is there for you to do?"

"We have to assure ourselves that Ramirez and Estavez are indeed quite dead."

"Along with a couple of hundred others!"

"Unfortunate, but there was no other way, I'm afraid," that cold, cruel voice added.

"How could you expect *them* somehow to be among the ones who might survive?"

"We have to be certain," the man said, in a half-growl. "We have to be certain that they will reveal *nothing!* And this is the only way to guarantee that. Besides, if either of the Bartlett kids survive, we can use them to get to the President's new National Security Advisor."

Bosworth started laughing again, only with a touch of pleasure this time.

"What is so funny?" the other man asked.

"They're nothing compared to what I've gathered together in my files. Can't you see that?"

Bosworth cleared his throat. Admitting mistakes to these men would give them a sign of weakness that they would *never* let him forget.

He had stumbled upon something that made him suspect that he had a mole in his office. A mole was government talk for a spy. Someone was pretending to be on his side but really worked for another individual politician or political party itself.

Certain files had a secret code of sorts. The pages were in a specific order, and only he knew the order.

Just minutes earlier, he found that order disturbed. Someone had not been so careful. Someone had—.

"Oh, you mean, Jeffrey Toland's snooping," the harsh voice snapped him out of his thoughts.

"Toland's the one?" Bosworth said, reacting with high-pitched alarm that he immediately regretted but couldn't suppress.

"Yes, he is. We have two men following him. He's with Andrew Bartlett."

"You *know* where to find him?"

"We know many things. Can it be that you don't realize this *by now?* We have men everywhere. Most human beings will sell their souls to anyone anywhere anytime if the circumstances are right. You of all people should know the truth of that."

"What do you want me to do?" Bosworth asked, not wanting to hear what the answer to that question was.

"Kill him."

Those words were spoken in a manner so matter-of-fact that the senator's blood was chilled.

"I won't do that," he replied. He knew, of course, that soon agents would arrive at his office, that he would submit himself to their custody, and that would be the end of it.

"You have no choice."

"I *do* have a choice. I can commit a murder, or I can refuse to do so."

"If you refuse, you will have other blood on your hands. And you will *never* get rid of the stains. This I can promise!"

"*Other* blood? What are you talking about?"

"Look, Bosworth, we know where your family is. You're no longer together with them, but I suspect you still care what happens to them."

"How are *they* connected with this?" Bosworth demanded.

"We have our best men watching every move your family makes. I will call a mobile phone number as soon as I hang up with you. I will call to say that you are going to do what *you* have been ordered to do. Or I will call to tell them what *they* must do."

"But why not someone else?" the senator wanted to know. "I have done everything else that you have ever asked. Surely you know that I am not the kind of man who could walk up to someone, and take a gun, and—."

"Security would never allow a complete stranger near Jeffrey Toland," the other man interrupted.

"But since he knows what is going on, why would he respond more positively to a culprit like me?"

"Because you will lie and tell young Toland that you have decided to cooperate with the Federal authorities."

Bosworth sucked in his breath, then immediately hoped that the other man hadn't noticed that he had done this.

"Are we clear about everything, S*enator* Bosworth? It is, as the expression goes, your call. What sort of message do I now leave with the men watching your family?"

Ten

The impact jolted Chad so much that he thought he would die that instant. And he prayed instinctively, asking the Lord to be with his father when the elder Bartlett was told what had happened.

But, as it turned out, Chad was about half conscious through the jetliner's plummeting dive from 5,000 feet. And, then, he continued in that same state, as the large plane hit a house, ripped right through it, jammed into another, and finally shuddered to a halt.

There had been wild, terrified screams from other passengers.

These were deafening in his ears.

Then darkness. But even then part of him was still aware, hearing, smelling.

Shattering sounds.

Maybe glass breaking somewhere. Crackling, sputtering sounds. Something on fire somewhere.

He heard voices, many voices, voices drifting out of the awful darkness.

Heat.

From the fire undoubtedly.

Along with the odor of leaking fuel, fuel upon which any fire would feed, and grow, and destroy.

Something wet, sweet in his mouth.

He knew he had to move.

But he couldn't. It seemed as though both legs were paralyzed, or no longer connected to him!

"I've got to get out of the plane," he shouted. "I think it's—."

On fire!

That would explain the heat, the sputtering, crackling sounds.

He tried again to move. Feeling had returned to his legs.

"Thank you, Jesus," he said. "Thank you, Lord."

Something was weighing down on his chest.

A piece of the plane? Someone's carry-on luggage knocked from its overhead storage bin?

He reached out . . . touched whatever it was . . . and pulled back instantly, his heart pounding.

Someone's head.

Someone's soft hair.

"I've got to open my eyes!" he shouted, as panic grabbed ahold of him. "I've got to see where I am, who this is."

Chad tried to command his eyelids to move as they should.

But they weren't obeying him as quickly as he had wanted.

At least that was how it seemed in the confused moments after the plane hit the ground and cracked open in dozens of places.

Thousands of pieces of metal and plastic every- where.

Sobbing.

A voice. Familiar.

A weak voice calling him, calling, calling, call-ing, "Chad, I'm hurt. I think some ribs are broken. Chad, I—." The voice faded away.

Chad Bartlett's eyes shot open then.

He saw a body on top of him, the face cut, the cheeks smudged with dirt.

Ryan.

It was Ryan!

Jeffrey Toland had asked to go along with An-drew Bartlett to the crash site, which was less than ten miles away from where they were.

"I'd like to help," he said earnestly.

Mr. Bartlett nodded appreciatively.

Ten minutes later, they were on the way.

Toland could see that his new friend's cheeks were wet with fresh tears.

"I admire you so much," he said to the older man.

"Why is that?" Mr. Bartlett asked.

"You aren't afraid of emotion. You risk your life for your country. You care about people. I know so many of the stories about you."

"Undoubtedly, a large percentage aren't true. There's a lot of hot air around these days."

"But some *are* true. And they show a man with *feelings,* sir, not a ruthless killing machine."

"God gave us the right kinds of feelings. What we do with them, what we turn them *into* is *our* responsibility."

"You're a Christian?" Toland interrupted.

"I am."

"The boys, too?"

"Very much so," Mr. Bartlett assured him.

"As a Christian, then, you obviously feel that you will be reunited with your wife in eternity."

"I do, Jeffrey, but that's where the emotion part is a little misleading. Because I *feel* a certain way should never be the reason for judging truth or falsehood. Emotions are temporary and can be manipulated.

"You see, I thank God that my belief in eternity is *not* based at all on any kind of fragile human emotion. If that were the case, during those times when I feel awfully discouraged about life, I might convince myself that there *isn't* any heaven, that *this* life is all I have. I mean, what a crushing, terrible reality that would be, Jeffrey."

Toland considered that for a moment, then: "Since I am a Christian also, I *want* to feel as you do. I *want* to think that life isn't all that I see around me, for what I see around me is pretty slimy these days."

"It's *always* been slimy, as you say, Jeffrey. There were corrupt politicians a hundred years ago, during the Civil War, and before that, in the American Revolution. Thousands of years earlier, Rome was filled to overflowing with them during the period of its decline.

"History has seen some rotten kings and, even, some popes, along with businessmen and others from every era."

"And now, today," Toland added in agreement, "we're heading toward another example of just what evil men are capable of doing. Isn't that it?"

Mr. Bartlett jerked his head around at that one, startled anew at the truth of what Toland had said.

"Yes, Jeffrey. But this kind of massive destruction goes beyond anything that even the Cartel could justify," he said. Andrew Bartlett was still trying to convince himself that anyone or any group could be responsible for such a thing. Somehow it was easier to think of it as a freak accident, even though he knew better.

"Forgive me, sir, but I do disagree. In my opinion, these guys definitely could have considered an act as monstrous as this one. If you were to look at it in their warped manner of thinking, it makes sense. They wanted to rid themselves of the threat represented by those hijackers, but without calling attention to themselves."

"I hope I never meet Richard Bosworth," Mr. Bartlett remarked. "I *pray* that I don't, for *his* sake. It was hard enough just talking to him on the phone."

"I doubt that Bosworth dreamed up something as extreme as this," Toland replied. "I see him as someone who has been corrupted, someone who has turned his back on what goes on at Forbidden River and elsewhere. There's no doubt about that. But he's not a man who could live with the nightmare of having participated in the—."

Toland cut off his final words.

But Mr. Bartlett added these in for him.

"—slaughter of possibly hundreds of innocent men, women, and children. Isn't that what you were going to say?"

Toland had to admit that it was.

"In the past fifteen minutes I've gone over and over in my mind," Mr. Bartlett confessed, "how I would react if, when we get to the crash site, I find that Ryan and Chad are . . . are dead?

"I would surely try to keep my emotions to myself, and act brave, and help out as much as I was needed. There will be many others from the agency present.

"Every one of of us have been trained to maintain self-control *whatever* the situation might be. And I can't let them think that they've failed with me, not after so many years. You see, that would be a terrible thing, and I . . . I must be sure that it doesn't happen. I—."

He pulled the car over to the side of the road.

"Jeffrey, would you kindly take over for me?" he asked, some quivering in his voice.

Toland did so without comment. There was no need for words. He knew the reason as soon as Andrew Bartlett had asked.

 # Eleven

Neither Ryan nor Chad were pinned down by torn metal.

Lord, Chad thought, *I need Your help desperately. Please make me strong enough to take my brother and get away from—.*

There was an explosion . . . more screams and moans, and cries of the injured.

A quick glance around the wrecked hull of the jetliner showed that other passengers hadn't been so fortunate.

Chad gently lifted Ryan off his chest and then stood, continuing to hold his now unconsious brother.

The two were still in the passenger's cabin. A section of the roof had been ripped away.

How can I do this alone? Chad wondered.

"I'll help," a voice said.

Roberto Estavez!

"Carlos?" Chad asked. "Is he—?"

"Dead," Estavez told him.

"I'm sorry."

"So am I. I'll miss Carlos more than you'll ever know. But let's get out of here or we won't survive either!"

Estavez was an older, bigger man. Chad, though tightly-muscled, with the build of a strong athlete, still had the smaller frame of a growing teenager. Estavez would have to be the one to lift Ryan up through the hole in the roof, as steadily as possible so that the unconscious fourteen-year-old wouldn't come in contact with ragged metal edges.

Chad climbed up first, avoiding any injury, and then reached out to grab his brother when Estavez hoisted him through the hole. The man then pulled himself up and out of the cabin.

"Praise God that you're here!" Chad said.

"It wasn't supposed to turn out like this," Estavez told him. He sounded like a man who was offering a deep and terrible confession.

"I don't understand."

"Later, kid. Let's get away from this plane now."

They managed to get Ryan down off the plane and carry him a few hundred feet or so from it.

The scene was like one out of a Hollywood disaster movie. People were screaming, running, bumping into one another. There was the sound of sirens from approaching emergency vehicles.

Then another explosion came from the plane, this one even shaking the ground underneath them. Instantly the jetliner was covered with yellow-red-orange flames spurting out from its engines and elsewhere.

"What a stupid accident," Chad said as the three of them rested on the cold ground in that dark and awful night. "I've heard about this kind of stuff happening but—."

"No accident," Estavez said.

"What do you mean? Of course it was. We were there when it happened, after all!"

"Arranged."

"Arranged? By who—."

Chad's eyes widened.

"How do you know such a thing?" he asked.

"I . . . I—," Estavez started to say, trying hard to spit it out.

He turned, looked directly at Chad.

"I was supposed to take care of Carlos after we landed."

"*You?*"

Chad filled with anger.

"You're on their payroll?"

Estavez nodded.

"What went wrong?" Chad asked. "Why was there such a drastic change of plans?"

"I guess they figured they couldn't take a chance. There's a lot at stake, billions that they can't risk losing. What Carlos knew, so did I. They felt that they had to eliminate both of us."

"But *this* way?"

"When you're pumping poisons into millions of people, a few hundred mean nothing."

Ryan was moaning.

"We've got to get help!" Chad stated the obvious.

Just ahead they could see the first ambulance.

"There!" he said, pointing.

"You stay here. I'll get the paramedics if somebody else hasn't claimed them already," said Estavez.

Seconds passed.

After nearly a minute, Estavez came back. With him were two men in white uniforms who looked as though they could carry the three of them and a couple of others besides!

They put Ryan on a stretcher and carried him to the ambulance, gently sliding him into the back.

"What's his name?" one of the paramedics asked.

"Ryan Bartlett," said Chad and started to climb in, but one of the men said no.

"He's my brother," Chad remarked. "I *am* going with him.

The men looked at one another and gladly let him climb into the ambulance beside Ryan.

Estavez wanted to go along as well.

"Stay here, Roberto," the other man said, his voice husky. "Help out! And, please, be careful!"

"Thank you," he replied, and turned back toward the burning plane as the ambulance quickly pulled away.

Stay here, Roberto. . . . The words began to sink in.

Estavez spun around and shouted, "You knew my name. How could you know my name?"

And please, be careful!

What should he be careful of? What in the world was this man he'd never met before trying to tell him?

Instantly Estavez started to run after the ambulance as it disappeared up the road.

"No! No" he said, nearly hysterical.

Gone.

The ambulance was not quite out of sight, but it was too far ahead for him ever to catch up with it.

He threw his head back, looking up at the night sky, and screamed, "Will the misery never end?"

Just then a small car pulled up near him.

Two men got out. Both of them rushed up to him.

"Can we help?" the older one asked.

"I'm okay," Estavez told him. Then he hurriedly explained what had just happened.

"You think they aren't really paramedics?" the man commented. "Impostors? Is that it?"

"Yes, *yes!* I think they were sent by—," Estavez started to tell him, then bit his lip. He didn't know who these strangers were. And it could be dangerous to say too much.

"It's all right," the older man said. "Say nothing just now. We're going after them."

"It's bad, mister, you don't know how bad."

"Oh, I do, young man," the man told him. "You can't imagine how much I know."

Estavez was becoming frustrated.

"You have *no idea* what's going on here, mister. It's ugly and dangerous; it's evil. You act as though you know a lot, and yet you don't really understand what you're talking abo—."

"Would it have anything to do with Forbidden River?" the man interrupted.

Estavez was astonished.

"How could *you* know?" he asked.

"I know. Let's just leave it at that. You're afraid of ending up in Forbidden River, or some American version of it. From what I hear, it should be renamed Murder River."

"That's true, mister and—."

Andrew Bartlett interrupted him.

"No more talk," he said. "My sons are on that ambulance or whatever it is. *We've got to hurry!* Which way did they go?"

Estavez watched him and the other man jump back into their car and speed off after the ambulance.

From what I hear, it should be renamed Murder River. . . .

Estavez considered those words, knowing how accurate they were. He remembered some of the ghastly sights he had seen when he worked in the Cartel's compound right beside Forbidden River.

It had always been called by that name because the area around it was so dangerous. It was filled with the most venomous snakes and spiders in the entire country, together with the crocodiles in Forbidden River itself. Only the hardiest natives who had been born and raised there ever managed to survive.

Until the Cartel moved in.

And they did so, with typical ruthlessness.

They sent in squad after squad of men whose job it was to clear the area that was needed for the compound. Many died, from snake and spider bites. Others were too careless near the water where the crocs waited in absolute motionlessness for the right moment to attack.

Finally, the compound was erected, surrounded by electric fences, land mines, and other traps. Day and night Cartel hencemen patrolled the grounds armed with the most powerful hand weapons.

Nearby was an airfield that also had been added. It was filled with attack helicopters, some fighter planes, and other vehicles.

They can fight a war there, if they have to do so, Estavez told himself, shivering at the stark images that bounded around in his mind.

Ryan was coming to, muscles all over his body aching painfully.

"Chad?" he asked, his vision not clear enough at first to tell who was sitting beside him.

"Yes," Chad said. "We're on the way to a hospital. You'll be all right, little brother."

Ryan turned his head slightly, looking at the interior of the apparent ambulance.

"In this?" he observed.

"Sure. It's an ambulance. What better transportation?"

"Chad . . ." Ryan started to say, still feeling very weak. "Look around you. It's not—."

And then he blacked out again.

At first Chad had no idea what his brother was getting at. He glanced about the interior.

And then it hit him.

There was the stretcher that Ryan had been placed on . . . but nothing else: no medical supplies, not even a first-aid kit.

But that wasn't all.

The interior showed an unacceptable amount of dirt in the floor corners and along the edges of the roof.

Unsanitary, Chad decided, admiring his brother's alert observation. *No ambulance would be as dirty as this.*

And there was no paramedic sitting with them, keeping an eye on Ryan's condition.

In front.

Both . . . were in front.

They hadn't checked Ryan at all.

Chad felt perspiration down his back.

I was so glad to get him inside that nothing registered at first about the ambulance itself. . . .

Chad peered through the plexiglass window separating the rear from the front.

One of the two men had his hand resting on top of a gun beside him on the seat.

A pistol with a silencer on it!

Twelve

Andrew Bartlett and Jeffrey Toland had the ambulance in sight, less than a quarter of a mile directly ahead of them. Roberto Estavez had remained behind, at the crash site.

"Look at the license plate!" Mr. Bartlett said. "They're very much amateurish in some things."

"What about the license?" Toland asked.

"It's not a correct code, Jeffrey. You see, a few years ago, the agency suspected some terrorist activity in which ambulances would be used.

"We managed to stop them from getting the real thing. So they put together their own. And they might have succeeded, because everything was in place, every detail."

"Except the license plate," Toland offered.

"Exactly right," Mr. Bartlett acknowledged.

The phony ambulance ahead turned a corner sharply.

Mr. Bartlett was not far behind it.

There had been a slight rain earlier in the evening. The asphalt highway was slippery in spots, a thin layer of ice beginning to form.

Both men saw the ambulance take the turn, then slide out of control into a thick oak tree.

"No!" Mr. Bartlett screamed.

He tried to stop his own vehicle, but the wheels would not grip anything as they, too, skidded on a patch of ice.

"Hold on, Jeffrey," he warned while he tried to keep the car from going out of control as the ambulance had just done.

He was unsuccessful.

The car didn't hit a tree, but it went off the road and over an embankment.

The door on Toland's side was sprung open, and he was tossed out. But Mr. Bartlett remained inside as the car flipped over and ended up hanging partway over a steep cliff, just above a housing development in the little valley below.

Toland was dizzy when he first tried to stand. But he steadied himself and ran as fast as he could to the car.

It was balanced dangerously on the edge.

Any sudden motion by either of them would surely send it crashing over the side of that cliff.

He hurried around to the driver's side.

Andrew Bartlett was face-down on the front seat, apparently flung in that direction, directly behind Toland himself, when the door was smashed open. There was no sign of blood anywhere.

"Sir, sir!" the younger man yelled.

Mr. Bartlett moved, groans coming from him.

"You may have some broken bones, sir," he said. "Please, stay where you are. No sudden motions. Please, sir, listen to me. Trust me. It's not just the possibility of your ribs being in bad shape."

He was shaking from the tension and tried to steady himself.

"If you move," he went on, "this car will fall over a very steep cliff. There are houses at the bottom. I'll get help!"

Mr. Bartlett managed to move one arm, his left, very slowly, motioning Toland on.

Toland started to climb up the embankment to the highway at the top when he heard voices.

He hesitated.

Loud voices.

He turned around, trying to discern the direction of the sounds.

Just then he heard twigs being broken underfoot.

He stooped down behind a bush.

A teenage boy.

Fighting a much larger man.

The boy managed to grab a rock and hit the man on the side of the head with it. But this did nothing more than daze him for a split second. The large man then reached out and grabbed the teenager's throat, pushing the boy to the ground and choking him.

Jeffrey Toland sprang forward, knocking the man to one side. As the other started to get back to his feet, Toland kicked him.

The man staggered, backward.

Near the car. Too near it.

He reached out for the rear fender, tried to brace himself against it, and both he and the car went over the cliff!

Chad rushed to the edge of the cliff, followed by Toland.

The car had hit a ledge halfway down the cliff. It was resting there, temporarily.

"Not for long, my friend," Toland said out loud. "That ledge doesn't seem to be very thick. Frankly I don't see how it can support that kind of weight for very long."

"Is there somebody in the car?" Chad asked, not knowing just what had happened or who was involved.

"You don't know?" Toland said, realizing at the same time that the teenager hardly could have known.

"Don't know what?"

"You're one of Andrew Bartlett's sons, aren't you?"

"Sure am. When my dad arrives, we'll—."

Toland reached out and grabbed Chad's ample shoulders, interrupting anything he had been going to say.

"We were following you, your father and I, when the car went out of control and—."

"Dad's down there . . . inside it?" Chad blurted out the words.

"Yes, he is. He's—."

Chad pushed past him and started to climb over the edge of the cliff.

"Don't," Toland warned him. "Your weight added to what's already on that ledge, it's . . . it's too dangerous."

"More dangerous is better than doing nothing."

"It isn't this time," Toland disagreed. "We're amateurs with this sort of thing. We've got to get help."

"Where? How?" Chad pointed out. "We have no phones."

Then he paused, snapping his fingers.

"Wrong!" he said. "That so-called ambulance at least had a transmitter. I think I can use it. And I can see if my brother is conscious or whatever."

"Go! I'll stay here."

Chad turned and ran back the way he had come. When he got to the ambulance, he saw something he could hardly believe. Resting on the asphalt outside the back compartment, the remaining kid-napper was bathing Ryan's head with a wet rag.

"He was moaning," the man said as he glanced at Chad. "But he's stopped now."

He saw the teenager's disbelieving expression.

"I . . . never wanted . . . to do this," he added. "We were told to find two Bartlett kids at the crash site. I thought right away that it was very . . . very wrong. But they . . . they have ways of getting anyone . . . yes, *anyone* to do what . . . they want."

"And how did *they* get to you?" Chad asked.

"My home is located in Fairfax, Virginia. My wife and my son are there right now."

"Your family is being threatened by members of the Forbidden River Cartel? Is that what you're getting at?"

"Yes!" the man admitted, his face contorted with anguish. "They're in the greatest possible danger."

"Help me," Chad told him honestly, "and my father will make sure you're protected."

"Your father? That's a big boast, young man. Forgive me if I wonder how you can back it up."

"I just can't tell you any of that right now, mister. But I'm going to try real hard to trust one of the two men who kidnapped my brother and me. Why don't you do the same with me? It shouldn't be anywhere near as difficult for you as it is for me!"

"Your father must be well connected. They didn't give us any details, just said to find two teenagers by the name Bartlett."

"Let's just say that he can pull the right strings to get you all the protection you need."

The man studied Chad for a moment, then nodded.

"The transmitter's still working. I've heard messages coming through on it. Go ahead. I'll stay here with your brother."

Chad thanked him and went around the side of the vehicle and hopped into the cab.

Ryan could have done this easily! he said to himself. *Here I am a real klutz with electronic equipment trying to use a transmitter to get help!*

But he managed, better than he could have predicted, getting through to the agency's special number, the one that had come in so handy in the past.

"Do nothing," the voice at the other end said after Chad had told him the problem. "You must not cause any motion whatever. We'll have someone on the spot in ten minutes or less."

Chad thanked whoever it was, then hung up, and hurried outside, to Ryan and their one-time kidnapper.

His name was Ramon Sarno.

"They are worse than anyone knows," Sarno said. "They are more powerful, more vicious."

"They can corrupt even United States senators," Chad added, recalling what he had learned while in flight.

"Much more than that," Sarno acknowledged. "They are experts at human nature. They find someone's weakness and move in on it, using it to their advantage."

"Sounds like Satan himself."

Sarno shuddered at that.

"You speak the truth," he added. "They are men but, often, they *act* like demons. They will show compassion, it seems, for their families and their friends. But let any of those people give signs of a conscience, of wanting to stop the selling of evil drugs, then even love for a wife, a son, a daughter, a friend will disappear in an instant."

His face was twitching.

"I am an example. I am an example of someone they can grab ahold of and force to act according to their every whim."

"Your family will have Secret Service agents at their doorstep only a little later than when help arrives here," Chad tried to assure him.

"But how can you say that? You are only a boy."

Chad blushed at that.

"A boy blessed by the Lord in so many ways, Ramon."

Sarno started to cry.

"I *have* prayed for help, you know. I have prayed often. I have begged God to help me and my loved ones."

"It seems to me that the Lord has heard you and acted," Chad said softly. He truly believed that this man's pleas to God were not the only ones that had been answered.

In minutes, a crane had arrived, equipped with a long metal cable from which hung a sturdy hook.

One of Andrew Bartlett's fellow agents had insisted upon doing the rescue work.

"He's saved my life more than once," the man said. "I owe him this. Nobody else gets the job."

Holding onto the cable, he was lowered to the edge of the car and was about to connect the hook to what seemed a sturdy section at the rear, the axle itself.

The car lurched, slipping another inch or two.

"Hold it!" someone shouted from above. "Around the side. Look!"

Andrew Bartlett apparently was thrown into the back seat when the car went over the cliff. The sedan's rear door opened slightly when contact was made with the ledge. And now Mr. Bartlett had crawled part way out of the car. Only his legs, from the knees down, remained inside.

"No, Andy, don't move anymore," the agent shouted. "Man, you should know better than that!"

Mr. Bartlett turned, looked up at him.

"I had to do something," he shouted back. "There's a fuel leak somewhere. This thing could—."

The two men were only inches apart.

The agent leaned his body weight against the cable, swinging it slightly toward the other man.

"Grab my hand, Andy!" he said, as he held on with his left hand, and stretched out his right arm.

The car lurched again, slipping further.

For a split second, Mr. Bartlett hesitated. Then, weak from injuries, he tried unsuccessfully to reach the outstretched hand.

"Again, Andy, again!" the agent shouted.

The man unbuckled his climber's safety belt, a risky move at such a height. But by doing this he was able to lean father away from the cable. Otherwise he'd never be able to reach his old friend.

There was nothing to hold him now except his own strength!

He closed his eyes for a quick prayer, then slipped down onto the hook itself.

"Now, old buddy, now!"

Mr. Bartlett gathered all the strength he had left and pushed himself up and toward the other man's hand, now less than an inch away.

He missed!

But managed to reach the hook.

The agent got ahold of him then, and pulled him up to a sitting position.

"Can you make it, Andy?" he asked.

"My sons! . . . are—are they okay?"

"They're going to be just fine," the agent reassured him.

Thank you, Lord, Mr. Bartlett prayed. Then he closed his eyes, very nearly passing out.

"Go first, Andy," he said.

He took off a second climber's belt from his well-worn leather holster and wrapped it around Mr. Bartlett's waist, fastening its metal clasp on the cable.

"Hug the cable with your legs. I'll be under you, acting as support."

Mr. Bartlett smiled.

"Haven't we been through something like this before?" he said.

"One way or the other, old pal," the agent said.

Just as they began the climb up from the ledge, flames started shooting out from under the hood of the car. An instant later, it exploded.

The agent's grip was knocked loose from the cable, and he started falling. Mr. Bartlett reached out to grab him. Their fingers touched, but that was all. And the agent shouted, "See you in heaven, dear friend," as he fell away, down into the valley below.

Mr. Bartlett, sobbing from the tragedy of losing the other man, clung to the cable. He was grateful for the safety belt his friend had provided, but he felt guilty over what this had caused.

See you in heaven, dear friend. . . .

Andrew Bartlett said good-bye as once again he started to lose consciousness.

Another man was getting ready to go after Mr. Bartlett. But Chad beat him to it.

"You're crazy, son," the tall agent said. I'm—"

"—stronger," Chad anticipated. "Are you so sure?"

"Of course."

"Because you've got ten years on me? All right, how many pounds do you bench-press?"

"About 250 maybe, but I don't keep at it."

Chad was smiling as he said, "I'm at 300, and I'm doing it three, sometimes four days a week!"

He was out onto the cable before anybody could stop him.

And he was halfway down when someone shouted something at him that chilled his blood.

"The crane's stuck! We were in such a hurry that we didn't check it out. *You've got to get him up on your own!*"

Chad almost froze midway along the cable, his mind going blank for a moment as the utter terror of where he was got to him.

The heat was getting to be fierce. Bushes and trees for hundreds of yards had caught fire from the explosion. Embers were floating like fireflies in every direction.

"Dad!" he yelled as he saw close up the paleness of his father's face.

"Son!" Mr. Bartlett said, his eyes half-closed.

"You can't fall, Dad," Chad told him. "Remember that. The climber's belt is on solid."

"But . . . we . . . both can . . . be roasted like . . . pigs on a spit!" Mr. Bartlett exclaimed, his voice hoarse.

"I'm going to get down onto the hook and push you from beneath. When we're up far enough I'll be able to get some traction on the cable itself. Then, as I swing from under you I want you to reach out and put your arms around my neck."

"Too heavy . . ." his father muttered.

"Look . . . I've already had that argument with somebody else. Trust me, Dad. Your weight is a piece of cake compared to what I've been lifting lately. Besides, there's no other way!"

Mr. Bartlett groaned assent.

Chad climbed down the cable, holding onto the opposite side from his father. He got to the large hook and was ready to push the man up a bit when he lost his grip on the cable.

He was able to grab hold of the hook just in time!

Chad needed all of his weight-lifting power to pull himself back up. He had nearly made it when a spark from the fire landed on the left leg of his jeans. He tried to shake it off but couldn't.

Oh, God, he prayed. *Oh, God, I need Your help again. I know You're not my private guardian angel or personal genie. And it might not be in Your will for Dad and me to survive this. But if it is, please, Lord, please help me as soon as You can.*

The searing heat seemed to reach right into his brain, and his grip on the cable was loosening.

His father and he glanced at one another, knowing that they were both close to dying. In that brief instant their eyes seemed to say so much: that neither should have any regrets . . . that they both had done their best.

His vision blurring, Chad reached out his hand to touch his father gently on the cheek.

"Oh, Dad," he started to say, thinking that they both would die in another moment or two. "Dad, I love you so much!"

Mr. Bartlett was about to speak when—.
Sirens!

Suddenly they both could hear some fire truck sirens, and Chad prayed that these were nearby.

Seconds later, he felt something for which he would never be more grateful than at that moment.

Water.

Lots of it.

Thirteen

The three Bartletts were rushed to Walter Reed Medical Center where they spent ten days recuperating. After being released, they went to the residence that had been provided for them by the government on a temporary basis until they could find a more permanent one. All three were looking forward to house-hunting.

Then began a nerve-wracking period of Senate confirmation hearings. It was nerve-wracking because some of the senators seemed to be quite eager to prove that Andrew Bartlett couldn't be as fine a man as he actually was. They often asked rude questions and showed no respect for his distinguished record.

The worst by far was a certain four-term senator from one of the New England states. He had white hair and a puffy face with thin, little veins close to the surface of his cheeks. This one tried to destroy Mr. Bartlett's reputation by suggesting that he had taken part in various attempted assassinations of foreign leaders over the years.

"Tell me, Mr. Bartlett. Don't you get a thrill out of your undercover work? Wouldn't you really like to have personally pulled the trigger on certain dictators?"

"All of us have rash desires from time to time, Senator," Mr. Bartlett answered. "All of us feel *tempted* even on a daily basis in one area or another. The key is whether we give in to those desires or, whether we successfully fight them. Day by day, I choose to fight. I choose *not* to tell lies to save my skin, as the expression goes."

He leaned forward, closer to the microphone in front of him.

"As a Christian, I have a still, small voice within me that I listen to, Senator," he said. "It is—."

"You listen to *voices?*" the New England senator interrupted. "Is that how you will advise the President of the United States on matters affecting the future of this nation and the world as a whole?"

He snorted in contempt and said, "As for me, I hear no such voices, Mr. Bartlett. I *need* no such voices."

A smile spread across Andrew Bartlett's face.

"What you say does not surprise me, Senator," he observed, speaking slowly, with great effect. "I was referring, for the most part, to my conscience. If there is no conscience, then *God* is silenced."

By Christmas that year, Andrew Bartlett had started his new job. A majority of the senators had eagerly confirmed him as the new National Security Advisor to the President of the United States. One after the other, they had not only praised him, but they had also taken the opportunity to condemn those colleagues who had attempted to damage his reputation.

"*They* are the ones who have been damaged, I assure you," remarked a senator from one state. "They have shown their true colors to the American public."

And so the hearings were over, and they could settle into a peaceful holiday season.

"Whatever happened to the hijackers and that one kidnapper, Dad?" Ryan asked, as they sat in the living room, looking at the beautiful Christmas tree they had just finished decorating.

"Estavez survived, his partner did not. He is now in a witness protection program."

"He helped out the authorities?" Chad asked.

"That he did. And so did Ramon Sarno. Both have provided information that goes along with what was found in the files Jeffrey Toland gave us."

"So the Forbidden River Drug Cartel has been stopped?" Ryan put in.

"No, son. It's been dealt some terrible blows, yes, and we should be grateful for that. But it's not stopped."

"Don't you wonder if it can *ever* be completely demolished, Dad?" Ryan asked.

"Yes, I don't know how, but we must keep fighting."

"How about Senator Bosworth?" Chad asked.

"He's going to a federal prison just after Christmas."

"How long will he be there?"

"It could be for the rest of his life, Chad. He's been convicted not just of bribery charges but of others that border on treason."

The phone rang.

It was Jeffrey Toland.

Mr. Bartlett's eyes widened.

After he had put the phone receiver back on its cradle, he turned to his sons and said, "The President and the First Lady wonder if we would like to join them for Christmas dinner."

"What!" Chad exclaimed in a very loud shout.

"Are you serious?" Ryan asked.

"I am. That was Jeffrey Toland."

"How did he find out?"

"He's now an aide to the President and the First Lady."

Mr. Bartlett was waiting for an answer to the invitation.

"Well, guys, can we fit it into our schedules?" he prompted.

And then the three of them broke out into uproarious laughter that felt good, very good indeed.

It was exciting, riding in a bulletproof government limousine and heading toward the White House. Jeffrey Toland was with them, and he was just as excited as they were.

"Amazing!" he said. "Amazing how in just a few months your life can change completely."

They all agreed.

"There hasn't been any new activity by the Forbidden River Cartel since the mid-air collision you guys were involved in," he said as he reached out and shook their hands in a gesture of triumph.

"Evil slumbers but threatens to awaken we know not when," Mr. Bartlett muttered.

"Heavy duty," Chad said kiddingly.

The rear gates to the White House were opened as they approached.

They got out of the limo and were in the process of being escorted into a side entrance. Then suddenly the vehicle exploded, sending debris from it all over White House grounds. Even a dozen windows, some of these a hundred years old, were shattered.

Vicious and unholy men had spoken brutally yet again from thousands of miles away, from an ancient and deadly place called Forbidden River. And Andrew Bartlett knew instantly that they would keep on doing so until—.

Oh, Lord, he thought prayerfully. *Oh, Lord, let me have the measure of strength and cunning I will need to take care of those I love so much.*

Once inside the White House, his body trembling, he reached out and hugged his sons while he still could. . . .

DON'T MISS THESE OTHER BARTLETT BROTHER ADVENTURES:

Sudden Fear

When Ryan Bartlett accidently intercepts a computer message, he and his brother are stalked by terrorists, who plan to destroy a nuclear power plant. (ISBN 0–8499–3301–3)

Terror Cruise

The Bartlett family embarks on a Caribbean cruise that is supposed to be a time of rest and relaxation, but instead becomes a journey into terror. (ISBN 0–8499–3302–1)

The Frankenstein Project

While visiting a friend in the hospital, Ryan and Chad Bartlett come face to face with secret scientific experiments and mysterious children. (ISBN 0–8499–3303–X)

ABOUT THE AUTHOR

Award-winning author Roger Elwood is well known for his suspense-filled stories for both youth and adult readers. His twenty-six years of editing and writing experience include stories in *Today's Youth* and *Teen Life* magazines and a number of best-selling novels for Scholastic Book Clubs and Weekly Reader Book Clubs. He has also had titles featured by Junior Literary Guild and Science Fiction Book Club. Among his most outstanding adult books is *Angelwalk*, a winner of the Angel Award from Religion in Media.